Explore the World of
Prehistoric Life

Text by Dougal Dixon
Illustrated by Tim Hayward

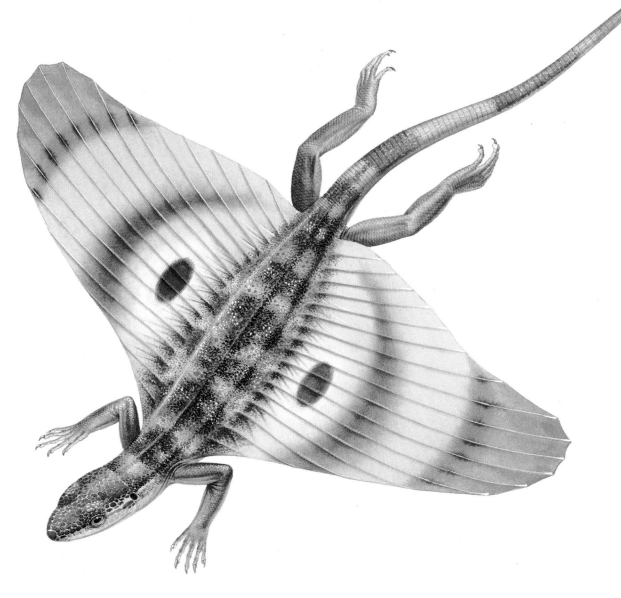

A GOLDEN BOOK • NEW YORK

Western Publishing Company, Inc., Racine, Wisconsin 53404

Contents

What were the first animals like?
Some of the oldest fossils reveal a world of fantastic
creatures that lived on the ocean floor in the
Cambrian period. Nature seemed to try out all
kinds of animal designs to see what would survive.
Although most of the animals were never seen
again, some animal designs gave rise
to descendants, such as half-
moon-headed trilobites
and worms, that fed
on sponges or
burrowed in
the mud.

Prehistoric Time Scale
This chart shows the different periods in our planet's history. It can be used to find out how long ago the animals and people in this book were living on Earth. The dates on the chart show when each period is believed to have begun — starting with the Precambrian, 4,600 million years ago.

Quaternary (Age of Mammals)	1.64
Tertiary (Age of Mammals)	65
Cretaceous (Age of Reptiles)	146
Jurassic (Age of Reptiles)	208
Triassic (Age of Reptiles)	245
Permian	290
Carboniferous	363
Devonian	409
Silurian	439
Ordovician	510
Cambrian	570
Precambrian	4,600
	Million Years Ago

5

Which was the first backboned animal?

The first backboned animals were fish. They were very simple creatures — little more than worms with backbones. *Arandaspis* has been found as a fossil in Ordovician rocks in Australia. It had no jaws and must have lived by sucking up mud from the bottom of the sea. In place of fins, *Arandaspis* had a paddlelike tail. Six inches long, it was covered with armor plates and scales. Swarms of *Arandaspis* probably wriggled around like young tadpoles. Its descendants developed fins that helped them to swim and jaws with teeth that helped them to eat. By the Silurian and Devonian periods, many kinds of fish lived in the oceans.

More about early fish

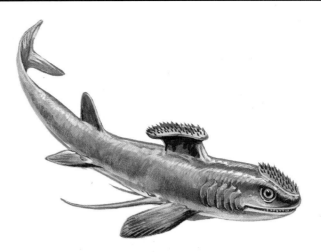

Sharks have remained almost unchanged to the present day. One shark from the Carboniferous period, *Stethacanthus*, had a fin covered with teeth on its back. Nobody knows what *Stethacanthus* used this fin for.

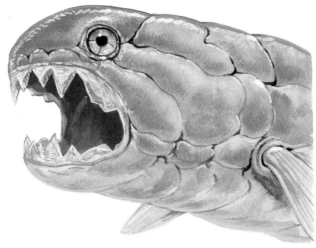

Dunkleosteus was a fish killer in the Devonian seas. It was a huge armored hunter, about 40 feet long. Its plated jaws were armed with bladelike teeth. The armored hunters, such as *Dunkleosteus*, did not survive after Devonian times.

Some fish, such as *Panderychthys*, developed lungs that could breathe air and pairs of muscular fins that could drag their bodies over the ground. This kind of fish could live out of the water for a short time. They eventually evolved into land-living animals.

Which animal first lived on land?

By the Silurian and Devonian periods, the first plants began to grow on land and the bare scenery started to turn green. The first land animals were insects, spiders, and scorpions. They left the water and were able to live among the first land plants. Soon amphibians evolved that could live both on land and in water. *Ichthyostega* was one of the first. It was about 3 feet long and had 8 toes on its hind feet. It still had a fish's skull and a fish's tail, like its ancestors. However, this land animal returned to the water to breed, and its young were water-living tadpoles.

More about early amphibians

By the Carboniferous period, there were many different kinds of amphibians. *Eogyrinus*, 15 feet long, cruised the murky waters of shallow swamps like a crocodile, looking for other amphibians and fish to eat.

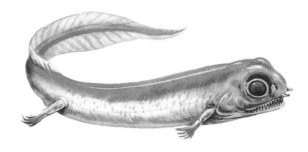

Some amphibians returned to a completely watery existence. Carboniferous *Crassigyrinus* was about 6 feet long and looked like a long eel, with big eyes for hunting in muddy swamp water. Its legs were too small to be of much use on land.

The swamps of the Carboniferous period became the dry deserts of the Permian period, and many land-living amphibians evolved there. One of these, *Platyhystrix*, was about 3 feet long. It was armored for protection and had a "sail" on its back.

What was the first reptile like?

Though the amphibians adapted well to their surroundings as land animals, they still needed to lay their eggs in water. Reptiles evolved during the early Carboniferous period and laid tough-skinned eggs on land. Each egg acted like a private pond for the baby animal. The first reptile, *Westlothiana*, was a lizardlike animal about 8 inches long. It scurried through the ferny undergrowth of the huge forests that would later be fossilized into beds of coal. *Westlothiana* was not the master of its domain, however. Other types of creatures, including centipedes as big as alligators, also hunted there.

More about early reptiles

How did early reptiles live?

Dimetrodon was a 6-foot-long hunter from the Permian period. It had a sail on its back, like that of the amphibian *Platyhystrix*. The sail was used to control *Dimetrodon*'s body temperature. In the morning the sail was turned to the sun to heat up the animal's blood and make it active. At midday the sail was held to the wind to cool off the animal.

How did early reptiles evolve?

By the end of the Permian period, descendants of *Dimetrodon* developed more complicated body-heating systems. Warm-blooded *Cynognathus* was able to regulate its body heat by the amount of food it ate. It was also covered in fur that kept its temperature at the same level all day.

What were plant-eating reptiles like?

Most of the early reptiles ate meat or insects. The plant eaters evolved later. They needed special teeth and large stomachs to digest the plant material, so they were usually bigger than meat eaters. *Scutosaurus*, a plant eater from the late Permian period, was the size of a cow.

Did some early reptiles fly?

During the Permian period, some early reptiles developed the ability to fly, or at least to glide. *Coelurosauravus* had ribs that grew out from the sides of its body. The ribs supported a pair of skin wings, giving it a foot-wide wingspan. This reptile probably glided from tree to tree, like a modern flying squirrel.

Did some early reptiles swim?

Although reptiles evolved to live on land, many later developed bodies that allowed them to return to live in the water. *Mesosaurus*, about 28 inches long, was a lake-living animal from the Permian period. It had webbed feet, a finned tail, and very fine teeth for straining tiny animals from the water.

Do any of these early creatures exist today?

Sometimes a creature's evolution was so successful that it has survived virtually unchanged until the present day. The turtles and tortoises are one such group. The earliest turtle, *Proganochelys*, from the Triassic period in Germany, had a shell that was almost identical to turtle shells found today.

How did the first dinosaurs evolve?

Imagine a crocodile out of the water. See how strong the back legs are and how heavy the tail is? These features enable the crocodile to swim. Now imagine this crocodile living on land. To catch its food, it would have to move quickly. The best way of doing this would be to run on its long hind legs. Its jaws and teeth would still be at the front, balanced by the tail behind. The dinosaurs evolved from crocodilelike ancestors precisely in this way. The earliest was the 12-foot-long *Herrerasaurus* from the middle Triassic period. It looked very much like a two-footed crocodile.

Which were the biggest meat eaters?

The meat-eating dinosaurs grew to be enormous. They hunted their prey with great teeth and claws. Some were over 40 feet long and preyed on the biggest plant eaters of the day. One of the biggest meat eaters was *Spinosaurus* from the early Cretaceous period. It had a long face with narrow jaws and a huge sail on its back — like a "great flag" that was 6 feet high. Like the early reptile *Dimetrodon* and the amphibian *Platyhystrix* before it, *Spinosaurus* probably used the sail to control its body temperature in the hot, dry conditions where it lived.

More about big meat eaters

Tyrannosaurus, which was about the same size as *Spinosaurus*, has always been regarded as the biggest meat eater that ever lived. It hunted in North America in the late Cretaceous period — the very end of the Age of Dinosaurs.

South America had its big meat eaters, too. *Carnotaurus*, which was more than 36 feet long, must have been a frightening threat to the plant eaters in late-Cretaceous Argentina. It had a strange, short face and a pair of horns, like those of a bull.

The smaller meat eaters were probably more active and ferocious than the giants. *Ceratosaurus* was only about half the size of *Tyrannosaurus*. Despite its size, *Ceratosaurus* probably survived by hunting in packs that stalked the forests of late-Jurassic North America for unfortunate plant eaters.

Which were the smallest meat eaters?

Stenonychosaurus, a small dinosaur from the late Cretaceous period in North America, was built for running, like a modern emu or ostrich. Unlike the much larger dinosaurs, its brain was very large. It had a pair of huge eyes, which scientists think enabled it to hunt by night, like an owl. We can imagine this creature stalking the early mammals and small reptiles through moonlit forests, pouncing on them and killing them with the claws on its toes.

More about small meat eaters

Deinonychus, from the early Cretaceous period in North America, was a vicious, wolf-sized dinosaur that hunted in packs. It could kill animals bigger than itself, tearing and slashing through thick skin with the huge claw on its toe.

Chirostenotes, from the late Cretaceous period in Canada, was about the size of a turkey. It had a short tail and very long arms and fingers with claws.

Avimimus was probably a slender, quick-footed dinosaur. It was built like an ostrich and could also run as fast as one — about 35 miles per hour— over the plains of late-Cretaceous Mongolia.

More about sea reptiles

How can an animal's body help it to swim?
Think of an eel — a long, snakelike fish that swims by throwing its body into big S-shaped curves. Some reptiles adopted this shape, too. *Pleurosaurus*, a 2-foot-long animal from the Jurassic and Cretaceous seas, was related to the modern tuatara reptile of New Zealand. It had a long, narrow body and tail, but its legs were too small to be used in swimming.

Did reptiles eat shellfish?
Placodus, from the Triassic seas of central Europe, looked somewhat like a big newt. It was about the size of a seal and had webbed feet and a flattened swimming tail. The short jaws had teeth that were made for crushing something hard, such as shellfish.

How can we recognize a fish eater?
Nothosaurus, which lived in Triassic seas all over the world, had long, narrow jaws that were armed with many sharp teeth. These were used for snatching and holding slippery prey — like fish. The webbed feet and finned tail helped it to swim after its prey.

How did ichthyosaurs evolve?
The ichthyosaurs were the most aquatic of the water-living reptiles. *Cymbospondylus*, from the middle Triassic period in North America, was about 30 feet long. It had paddles and a long, eel-shaped body, similar to some of the smaller swimming reptiles.

Which reptiles were like whales?
The pliosaurs, related to the plesiosaurs, had huge heads and short necks. *Kronosaurus*, from the early Cretaceous seas of Australia, was over 50 feet long and was a very good swimmer.

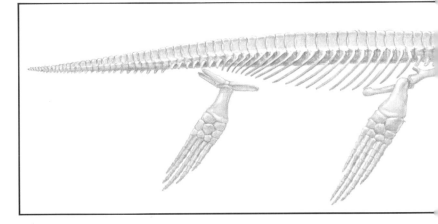

What were the later ichthyosaurs like?

The ichthyosaurs, such as *Ichthyosaurus* itself, soon developed into fishlike or dolphinlike animals. *Ichthyosaurus* had a streamlined body, a swimming fin on its tail, a stabilizing fin like that of a shark on its back, and a set of flippers. It also had pointed jaws full of fish-catching teeth.

What was a plesiosaur?

"A snake threaded through the body of a turtle" is how one early scientist described a plesiosaur when he studied its skeleton. It had a flattened body with paddle limbs and a very long neck. *Hydrothecrosaurus* was about 50 feet long, more than half of which was its neck. The plesiosaurs evolved from animals related to *Nothosaurus*.

What replaced the ichthyosaurs?

The ichthyosaurs died out before the end of the Age of Reptiles. Their place was taken by a group of sea-living lizards called the mosasaurs. These were related to the modern monitor lizard, but had fins and paddles and grew to be about 28 feet long. *Tylosaurus*, from the late Cretaceous period, was a typical mosasaur.

What were the ancient turtles like?

Archelon was as big as a rowboat, paddling slowly in the late Cretaceous seas. Like the modern leatherback turtle, it did not have a hard shell but instead had a thick skin that covered its bony ribs. It also probably existed on a diet of jellyfish.

Skeleton of a plesiosaur

How tall were some dinosaurs?

Just as the long neck of the giraffe enables it to browse high up in the trees, the necks of certain dinosaurs allowed them to do the same. The best known of these dinosaurs is *Brachiosaurus*, which lived in late Jurassic times. Its front legs were longer than its hind legs, making the shoulders high. Its long neck reached up from the shoulders so that its head was held over 40 feet above the ground — as high as a four-story house. However, even this was not the tallest of the dinosaurs. Scientists have found the huge bones of animals that may have been a dozen feet taller than *Brachiosaurus*.

Which were the longest dinosaurs?

Some of the big plant eaters were long rather than tall. *Mamenchisaurus*, from late-Jurassic China, was 83 feet long. Its neck was 49 feet long and was made up of 19 vertebrae, which makes it the longest neck of any animal. The muscular hips of *Mamenchisaurus* may have enabled it to rear on its hind legs to reach the highest branches in search of food. Like the other long-necked plant eaters, *Mamenchisaurus* lived in herds, wandering across wooded river plains, eating leaves from trees. Because they traveled in herds, they were able to protect their young from the fierce meat eaters that lived in China at the time.

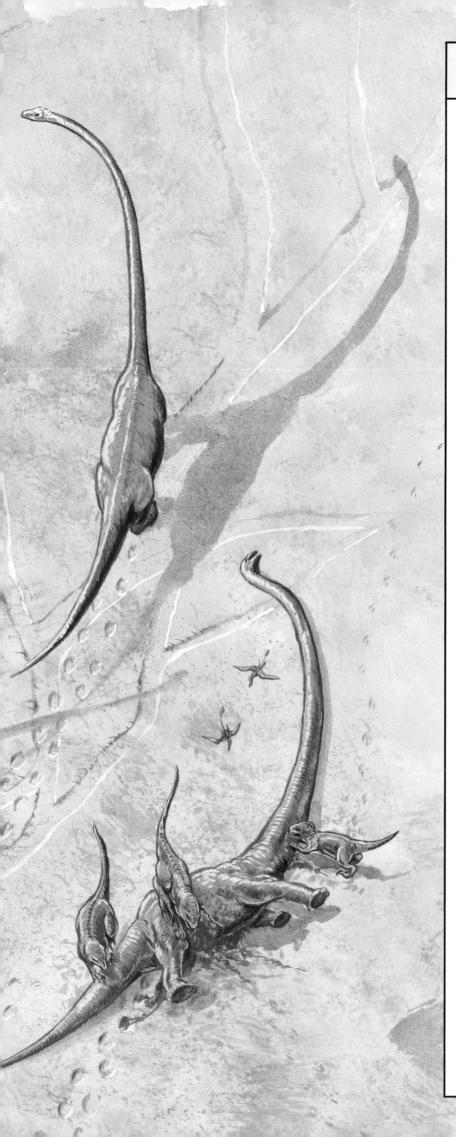

More long-necked dinosaurs

The plant eaters had many ways of defending themselves against the hunting meat eaters. *Diplodocus* had a long, whiplike tail that was probably used as a weapon to strike at any approaching predators.

Apatosaurus could have used its weight as a weapon. If it reared up on its hind legs, it could stomp down on any *Ceratosaurus* that came too close. The heavy claw on its forefoot could inflict severe damage.

Shunosaurus was a small animal for the long-necked group — only about 16 feet long. However, its tail seems to have had a club that could have been swung at the head of an attacker.

Which plant eaters built nests?

The first plant-eating dinosaurs walked on four legs, unlike the two-footed meat eaters. The two-footed plant eaters that evolved later had specially shaped hip bones and tails to allow them to balance on their hind limbs, particularly when running. The most successful of these dinosaurs were the late-Cretaceous duckbills. *Maiasaura* was one of these. It lived in herds, building nests in riverbanks and looking after its young — just like a bird.

More about plant eaters

Scutellosaurus, from the early Jurassic period in North America, was one of the first four-footed plant eaters to occasionally rear on its hind feet. It was not very big — about the size of a large dog — and it was covered in rows of bony plates.

One of the fastest of these dinosaurs was 7-foot-long *Hypsilophodon*, from the early Cretaceous period in England. It was built to be a sprinter — a kind of dinosaurian gazelle.

Ouranosaurus resembled the duckbills, such as *Maiasaura*, but it had a sail down its back. It was 23 feet long and lived in West Africa in the early Cretaceous period.

What were back plates used for?

Some descendants of the two-footed plant-eating dinosaurs became four-footed again. This was because they developed armor or ornamentation of some sort, and they needed all of their feet on the ground to support the extra weight. The stegosaurs, such as *Stegosaurus*, evolved this way. We can tell that they evolved from two-footed animals because their front legs were shorter than their hind legs. *Stegosaurus* had a double row of bony plates sticking up from its back. These were covered with skin or horn and may have been used to regulate the animal's body temperature, like the back fins of many other animals, or used as armor for defense.

Which dinosaurs had the most armor?

When the huge meat eaters, such as *Tyrannosaurus*, or the packs of vicious hunters, such as *Deinonychus*, stalked the forests, the plant-eating dinosaurs had to run away or defend themselves. The ankylosaurs were plant-eating dinosaurs that developed thick, heavy back armor as protection. One of these, *Euoplocephalus*, had an armored box for a skull, a back studded with stumpy knobs and plates, and a stiff tail that ended with a bony club. That club could be swung with shattering force against the legs of an enemy.

More about ankylosaurs

One of the earliest armored dinosaurs was *Scelidosaurus,* which lived in early Jurassic times. Its cow-sized body was studded with parallel rows of bony knobs, although it was not very heavily armored. Ankylosaurs evolved from *Scelidosaurus* or something similar to it.

Not all ankylosaurs were huge. *Struthiosaurus* was the smallest, measuring only 6 feet long — not much bigger than a large sheep.

Panoplosaurus was a heavily built ankylosaur. It had no club on its tail, but protected itself with the huge spines that stuck out at its sides. When a big meat eater attacked, it could crouch on its belly and be perfectly safe.

Why did some dinosaurs have horns?

The armor and weapons of some dinosaurs were concentrated on the head. The skull swept backward and formed a broad, bony frill around the neck. This could have been used as armor to protect the neck and body when facing an enemy. It could also have been used for display, like a peacock's tail. These dinosaurs also had horns on their faces. *Triceratops* is the most famous horned dinosaur. It fed on the leaves of palmlike cycad trees and migrated in small groups from time to time to find new feeding grounds. Triceratops locked horns and fought with each other to determine the leader of the group.

More about horned dinosaurs

Three-horned *Chasmosaurus* had an enormous bony frill, like a large sail. There were gaps in the bone, which would have made it lighter to carry. A frill as broad as this was probably brightly colored and used for display.

Styracosaurus had one massive horn on its nose. The edge of its frill was decorated with a series of spikes, pointing up and back, that made the frill appear much larger.

Pachyrhinosaurus was an oddity — a horned dinosaur with no horn on its nose; instead, it had a bony knob! These horned dinosaurs lived in North America at the very end of the Cretaceous period.

How did pterosaurs and birds differ?

Pterosaurs were flying reptiles that ruled the sky during the Age of Dinosaurs. They had broad, leathery wings supported by long "fingers." At this time, birds began to evolve from small meat-eating dinosaurs. Birdlike *Archaeopteryx* represents a halfway stage between dinosaurs and birds. *Archaeopteryx* still had jaws with teeth but no beak yet. Its wings had clawed fingers, and it had a long, dinosaurlike tail. But unlike the pterosaurs, *Archaeopteryx* had wings made of feathers. It lived on islands that existed in Germany in late Jurassic times.

More about early birds

Once *Archaeopteryx* had evolved, other kinds of birds developed. In early Cretaceous rocks in China, the fossils of the sparrow-sized bird *Sinornis* were found. It was an ordinary bird, with perching feet and a bird's tail, although it still had teeth and claws on its wings.

As they evolve, birds sometimes lose their powers of flight and take up a ground-dwelling life — especially on open plains. Today's ostrich and emu are examples. The hen-sized flightless bird shown here lived on the plains of Argentina in the late Cretaceous period.

Compsognathus, one of the smallest of the dinosaurs, was just like *Archaeopteryx* without any feathers. The two are so similar that we can be sure that birds and dinosaurs are related.

More about pterosaurs

How did pterosaurs evolve?
Scientists think that the ancestors of pterosaurs were small two-footed running reptiles that lived in the Triassic period. The dinosaurs may have had the same ancestors. *Dimorphodon*, with its big head, was an early Jurassic form of pterosaur from England.

How did pterosaurs fly?
It was once thought that pterosaurs just held out their wings and glided. Now we know that they flapped their wings, like birds. Some, such as *Rhamphorhynchus* from late-Jurassic Germany, had long, narrow wings and used the paddle on its tail to steer through the air.

Which was the biggest flying creature?
Quetzalcoatlus was a pterosaur that had a wingspan of about 36 feet — about the same wingspan as that of a small airplane. This would make it the biggest animal ever known to fly. It probably did not flap very much, but instead glided in the warm, rising air above North America in the late Cretaceous period.

Did pterosaurs have scales?

Some very detailed fossils have been found that show that pterosaurs were covered with hair. This suggests that they were warm-blooded. *Pterodactylus*, shown at left, from the same time and place as *Rhamphorhynchus*, had broad wings and a short tail.

How did the tailless pterosaurs steer?

Many pterosaurs had vanes or crests on their heads or jaws, which may have helped them to steer while flying. *Tropeognathus*, from the early Cretaceous period in Brazil, had a crest on its nose and another under its chin.

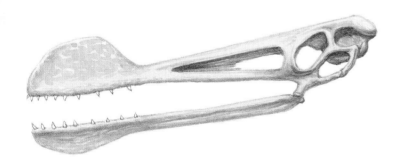

Did pterosaurs eat shellfish?

Dsungaripterus, from the early Cretaceous period in China, had forcepslike jaws for picking up shellfish and flat, strong teeth at the back of its mouth for crushing them. It had a wingspan of about 10 feet.

What did pterosaurs eat?

Dimorphodon was probably a meat eater, while *Pterodactylus* may have caught fish. *Pterodaustro*, from the late Jurassic period in South America, had long jaws filled with fine, comblike teeth. It probably strained tiny creatures from the water, as modern flamingos do.

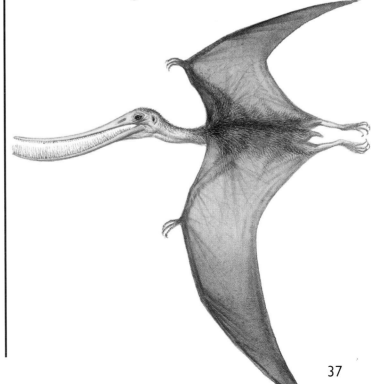

How did the Age of Reptiles end?

After 120 million years, the Age of Reptiles came to a sudden end. We do not know why, but there are many theories. One of the most popular is that the Earth was struck by a large meteorite, a swarm of comets, or something else that fell from outer space. The blast sent millions of tons of steam, dust, and smoke up into the atmosphere. This became a blanket of smog that spread around the world, cut off all the sunlight, and killed the plants. After several months without sunlight or food, the dinosaurs starved. When the smog lifted, new plants grew again, but the dinosaurs were gone forever.

More about the end of the reptiles

Other scientists believe that the Age of Reptiles may have ended gradually. The positions of the lands and seas were changing at that time. This would have caused the climate to change. It is possible that the dinosaurs would not have been able to adapt quickly enough.

Not all of the reptiles died out. Even though the dinosaurs, the pterosaurs, and the various swimming reptiles have gone, we still have the crocodiles, turtles, snakes, and lizards.

Mammals evolved at the same time as the dinosaurs, but they remained small, mouselike creatures, while the dinosaurs were the rulers. After the Age of the Reptiles, however, the mammals became dominant on Earth.

More about early mammals

Did any of the mammals fly?
When the pterosaurs had died out, some mammals took to the air and evolved into bats. *Icaronycteris* was an early bat, almost identical to ones we see today.

What did the ancient mammals eat?
Various kinds of mammals evolved and ate many different kinds of food. *Coryphodon*, for example, fed on water weeds, like the modern hippopotamus. It evolved a stout body with broad feet to anchor it in muddy water. It also developed tusks that could rake up the weeds from the river bottom.

Were there different mammals in Australia?
Today there are many animals that are unique to Australia. Because Australia is geographically isolated from the rest of the world, kangaroos, koalas, and wombats all evolved there and nowhere else. During the Age of Mammals, *Diprotodon* was a kind of gigantic wombat, the size of a bear, that lived only in Australia.

When did elephants evolve?
About halfway through the Age of Mammals, the forests began to be replaced by grasslands, and grass-eating mammals evolved. These were mostly running animals, such as antelopes and horses, but the elephants also developed. There were many different kinds, including *Amebelodon*, which had broad tusks shaped like shovels.

Which mammals lived only in South America?

South America was a big island throughout most of the Age of Mammals. Creatures evolved there that evolved nowhere else. *Megatherium* was a ground sloth as big as an elephant. Some mammals moved between North and South America when a land connection developed.

What preyed on these mammals?

Plant-eating mammals evolved quickly, at the same time as the meat eaters that killed and ate them. The first group of meat eaters were creodonts. Weasellike creodonts ate the small animals, and tigerlike creodonts ate the big ones. *Hyaenodon* was a wolf-sized creodont that ate the medium-sized mammals.

Did all the early mammals survive?

A lot of the early mammals that evolved soon after the Age of Reptiles did not survive. One of these was *Arsinoitherium*, a big rhinoceroslike animal with a pair of huge horns on its nose.

Which mammals lived in the sea?

After the Age of Reptiles, mammals developed that could live in any environment. Some even returned to the sea and evolved into whales. *Basilosaurus*, with a name like a dinosaur, was an early whale that had a 49-foot-long body. It looked like a sea serpent.

Which mammals were the best hunters?

For the first half of the Age of Mammals, the creodonts were the main meat eaters. Then they died out, and the modern meat eaters — the animals we call the carnivores — took over. The cat family is probably the most adaptable carnivore group today. Many kinds of cats evolved — adapting to hunt many different kinds of prey. The biggest cats were the saber-tooths from the Quaternary period, such as *Smilodon*. These had huge, saberlike teeth in the upper jaw, and massive neck muscles that enabled them to drive the head downward to deliver a killing blow. These fearsome beasts preyed on elephants. Only the saberlike teeth could penetrate the thick elephant skin and inflict a wound that would be fatal.

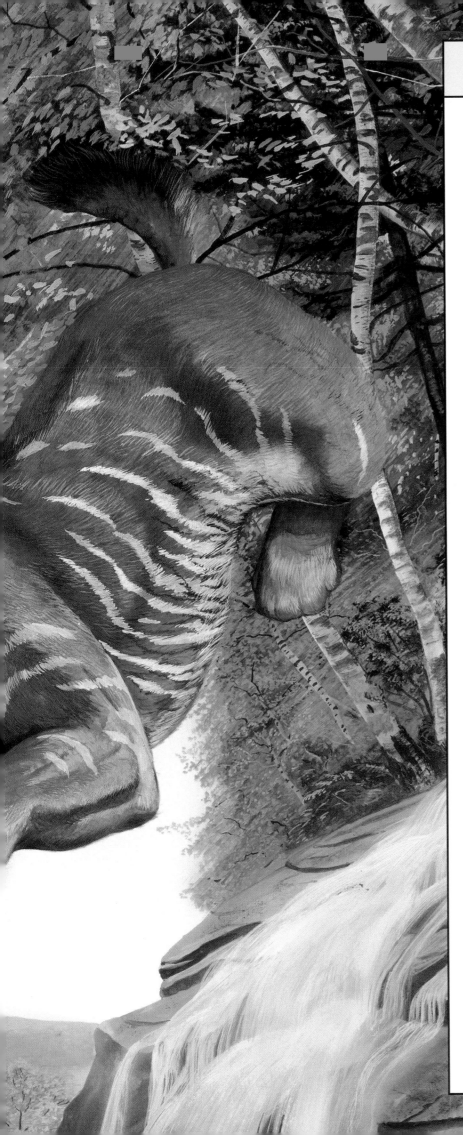

More about carnivores

Potamotherium, from the Tertiary period, was an early kind of otter, adapted to hunt fish in the water. With its long body and streamlined shape, it was typical of the carnivore group that contains the weasels and stoats.

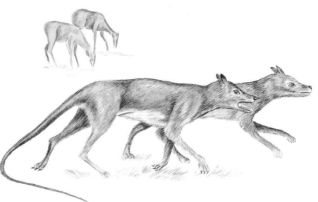

Dogs evolved at the same time as the grasslands. With their long legs, they could run down the swift grassland animals, like the antelopes. *Daphoneus*, from the Tertiary period, was an early dog with long, greyhoundlike legs.

A few carnivores took up a vegetarian way of life — or at least had a mixed and varied diet. *Chapalmalania*, from the same period as *Daphoneus*, was a kind of raccoon, but it looked something like a giant panda.

When did humans appear on Earth?

At the very end of the Age of Mammals, the first humanlike creatures, or hominids, appeared. Modern people — in many ways like us — are known to have existed some 40,000 years ago, during the Ice Age. These people probably painted the pictures that can still be seen today on the walls of caves in France and Spain. Most of the cave paintings are of animals, such as bulls, horses, lions, and deer, but there are occasional pictures of people. It is from pictures like these and from the study of fossils that we know about our ancestors.

Index

AN ILEX BOOK
Created and produced by Ilex Publishers Limited
29-31 George Street, Oxford, OX1 2AY

Main illustrations by Tim Hayward/Bernard Thornton Artists
Other illustrations by Steve Kirk, Denys Ovenden

DEP. LEG. B-10.386-92